Vroom!

HOT SUVS

MERCEDES AMG G 65

TABLE OF CONTENTS

AMG

The first modern car, built in 1901 and named after Mercedes Jellinek.

THE BEST OR NOTHING

Mercedes-Benz makes **luxury** vehicles. They created the first modern car, the Mercedes, in 1901. It began a fantastic history that reflects the company motto: "The best or nothing."

The Mercedes AMG G 65, powerful and **durable**, ranks among the company's most interesting vehicles. Many think it's the world's greatest sport utility vehicle (SUV).

The first Mercedes was named after Mercedes Jellinek. She was the daughter of race-car driver Emil Jellinek, who helped create the design of the first Mercedes. Her name became part of the company, along with Carl Benz.

Mercedes-Benz is **responsible** for many firsts. Those include the motorcycle (1885), automobile (1886), and truck (1896). The German company has a history of making history!

Mercedes-Benz partners with racing engine company AMG to create Mercedes-AMG vehicles that are high-performance, such as the G 65.

Karl Benz (sometimes spelled Carl)
1844 – 1929

The very first car had three wheels! Called the "Patent-Motorwagen," the car was made by Karl Benz. His wife, Bertha Benz, proved it could work by driving the car 120 miles (193 kilometers) with her two sons. She took them to visit their grandmother in Pforzheim, Germany.

Bertha Benz
1849 – 1944

CREATION OF THE G 65

Mercedes-Benz created the G 65 to make vehicles for off-road drivers. No other SUV looks like the G 65. The outer style hasn't changed much since the first G-class was produced in 1979.

The G 65 can handle any terrain. The "G" stands for the German word *gelandewagen*, which means "cross-country vehicle."

The **distinctive** design starts at the front with a chrome grille adorned with the famous three-pointed Mercedes-Benz star logo.

The sons of Gottlieb Daimler, one of the engineers who created what would become Mercedes-Benz, remembered their father had used a star as a symbol on his inventions. The company started putting the three-pointed star on all vehicles in 1910. It remains there to this day.

The rear has a swinging door and huge cargo area. A spare tire sits under a stainless-steel cover. It's an SUV that can take the family to the store or on an African safari!

AMAZING POWER

Mercedes-AMG engineers gave the G 65 the most powerful engine possible. The twin turbo, V12 engine produces an amazing 630 horsepower.

The G 65 engine produces an **incredible** 738 pound-feet (1,000 Newton-meters) of torque, which spins wheels faster. The G 65 goes from zero to 60 miles (96.5 kilometers) per hour in just 5.2 seconds.

The *G*-class has such a great reputation for handling every kind of terrain that 63 different armies have used it. Mercedes-Benz has an agreement to make the vehicles for NATO—the North Atlantic Treaty Organization—until at least 2025.

Each twin turbo, V12 engine in the G-class is handcrafted and signed by an AMG engineer.

COMFORT AND STYLE

Mercedes-Benz interiors are known for beauty. That includes the G 65. Leather seats offer comfort. Inside lights make it easy to see at night.

It also features cool technology. You can even start a G 65 remotely!

You can start a G 65 with the key above, or use the Mercedes remote start app on your smartphone.

Mercedes-AMG pays attention to sharp details. These include the "V12 Biturbo" badge, an AMG emblem on the gear shift, and illuminated door sill panels.

The Nappa leather has diamond-pattern stitching. Every seat is heated, as is the steering wheel. Why? Because it's a Mercedes.

Mercedes G-Class Timeline

In some markets, the G-class is sold as a "Puch G."

1970s: Mercedes partners with Steyr-Daimler-Puch of Austria to make the *gelandewagen*. The "G" is tested in the Sahara Desert and Arctic Circle.

1979: The first G-class is produced. It's a rugged vehicle intended for the military and forestry services.

1983: A G-class vehicle wins the Paris-Dakar Rally, a tough off-road **endurance** test.

The Paris-Dakar Rally crossed the Ténéré desert in Africa for the first time in 1983.

1980: Mercedes builds a G-Class vehicle for Pope John Paul II called the "Popemobile."

1981: Mercedes makes the "G" more pleasing for regular drivers, including air conditioning and electric windows.

Pope John Paul II rides in the Popemobile.

The Popemobile may be the most famous Mercedes-Benz belonging to a V.I.P., according to the Mercedes-Benz History Museum website. Other famous Mercedes drivers included Princess Diana, Jay Leno, and Michael Jackson.

The Popemobile inside the Mercedes-Benz Museum in Stuttgart, Germany

1989: Gunther and Christine Holtorf begin traveling the world in a G-Class they call "Otto." They cover an amazing 557,370 miles (897,000 kilometers). The vehicle never breaks down.

1993: Mercedes-Benz and AMG begin making cars together. AMG adds performance racing engines to G-Class vehicles.

1996: Mercedes makes a convertible version of the G-class that ends in 2013. The unique SUV remains popular.

2001: Mercedes begins selling G-Class vehicles in the United States.

A military fleet of Mercedes Interim Fast Attack Vehicles sits ready for duty.

In 2005, the U.S. military ordered more than 150 G-classes to replace outdated desert patrol vehicles. Mercedes-Benz also decided to introduce a new version of the G-class to the U.S. market called the Grand Edition.

2013: The G 63 6x6 becomes popular with **sheikhs** in the Middle East. With three axles and six tires, it's perfect for desert driving.

2017: Mercedes announces that, for now, they will only make the G 65 for law enforcement, military, and by special order.

G 63 6x6

The inside of the G 63 6x6 is as cool as the outside.

G63 AMG
AMG

2018: Mercedes-Maybach G 650 Landaulet is released. This ultimate "G" has an open top and seats that recline into sleeper beds.

The Landaulet is the ultimate vehicle for rugged adventures.

MAYBACH
des-Maybach G 650

The Mercedes-Benz Museum

A model race track with classic cars in the Mercedes-Benz Museum.

The Mercedes-Benz Museum in Stuttgart, Germany, has exhibits that **showcase** classic Mercedes cars, race cars, SUVs, ambulances, and even garbage trucks!

Among the collection are the original G-class Popemobile and Otto. As Mercedes-Benz says, "Where there's a G, there's a way."

GLOSSARY

distinctive (di-STINGK-tiv): making a person or thing different from all others

durable (DOOR-uh-buhl): tough and lasting for a long time

endurance (en-DOOR-uhns): the ability to do something difficult for a long time

incredible (in-KRED-uh-buhl): unbelievable or amazing

luxury (LUHK-shur-ee): something expensive that is nice to have but that you do not really need

responsible (ri-SPAHN-sub-buhl): being the cause

sheikhs (shayks): a sheikh is the head or chief of an Arab family

showcase (SHOH-kase): to display something or someone boldly and elaborately

INDEX

SHOW WHAT YOU KNOW

1. In what country was Mercedes founded?
2. Where does the name Mercedes come from?
3. What type of engines does AMG make?
4. What was the name of the first automobile, made by Carl Benz in 1886?
5. What type of cover is over the spare tire on the G 65?

FURTHER READING

Adkins, Jan, *Bertha Takes a Drive: How the Benz Automobile Changed the World*, Charlesbridge, 2017.

Cockerham, Paul H., *Mercedes-Benz: German Engineering Excellence*, Mason Crest, 2017.

Long, Brian, *Mercedes-Benz G-Wagon: 1979 – 2015*, Veloce, 2016.

ABOUT THE AUTHOR

Kevin Walker is the author of books about cars, science, and technology. He also writes about politics, film, and books. He likes books and cars the best. He's never owned a Mercedes, but he once owned (and loved) another German car—a 1971 Volkswagen Beetle.

Meet The Author!
www.meetREMauthors.com

www.rourkeeducationalmedia.com

PHOTO CREDITS: PHOTO CREDITS: All photos © Blue Door Education except cover © breif bluesky; Header art © Petrosg; speedometer art © didis both from Shutterstock.com; page 4 inset © MartinHansV; page 8-9 © Bahnfrend https://creativecommons.org/licenses/by-sa/3.0/deed.en; page 12-13 © Miro Vrlik Photography—Shutterstock.com; page 18 © High Contrast https://creativecommons.org/licenses/by/3.0/de/deed.en ; page 18-19 blue map © dikobraziy—Shutterstock.com, map showing desert location © En rouge and https://creativecommons.org/licenses/by/3.0/de/deed.en desert photo © Rusla Ruseyn—Shutterstock.com; page 20 pope mobile inset courtesy of Kancelaria Premiera, page 20-21 pope mobile © Benjamin B—Shutterstock.com; page 22-23 © Milhouse35 https://creativecommons.org/licenses/by-sa/3.0/deed.en inset © CEFICEFI https://creativecommons.org/licenses/by-sa/4.0/deed.en; page 26-27 © Alexander Migl https://creativecommons.org/licenses/by-sa/4.0/deed.en , inset © Matti Blume https://creativecommons.org/licenses/by-sa/4.0/deed.en ; page 28-29 © aldorado—Shutterstock.com; interior shot of museum © tichr—Shutterstock.com,

Edited by: Keli Sipperley

Cover design by: Rhea Magaro-Wallace

Library of Congress PCN Data

Mercedes AMG G 65 / Kevin Walker
(*VROOM!* Hot SUVs)
ISBN 978-1-64156-479-3 (hard cover)
ISBN 978-1-64156-605-6 (soft cover)
ISBN 978-1-64156-719-0 (e-Book)
Library of Congress Control Number: 2018930699

Rourke Educational Media
Printed in the United States of America, North Mankato, Minnesota